For Susie

First published in the United States 1992
by Dial Books for Young Readers
A Division of Penguin Books USA Inc.
375 Hudson Street
New York, New York 10014

Published in Great Britain 1991
by Methuen Children's Books
Text copyright © 1991 by Harry Yoaker / Simon Henwood
Pictures copyright © 1991 by Simon Henwood
All rights reserved · Printed in Singapore
First Edition
1 3 5 7 9 10 8 6 4 2

Library of Congress Cataloging in Publication Data
Yoaker, Harry.
The view / by Harry Yoaker ; pictures by Simon Henwood.
p.   cm.
Summary: Through a spirit of cooperation, a neighborhood
is saved temporarily from the adverse effects of an architectural
and environmental disaster.
ISBN 0-8037-1105-0
[1. Cooperativeness—Fiction. 2. Neighborliness—Fiction.]
I. Henwood, Simon, ill. II. Title.
PZ7.Y72Vi 1992 [E]—dc20 91-13353 CIP AC

THE VIEW

Harry Yoaker & Simon Henwood

With pictures by Simon Henwood

Dial Books for Young Readers  NEW YORK

Once upon a time there was a little group of houses that all looked the same.

Each house had the same number of doors and windows, and an identical garden and garden gate.

The only thing that was different about each house was the view from the windows. Each house had a completely different, but equally beautiful view. There were mountains and valleys, fields and forests, and in the distance the ocean.

One day the man who lived at house Number 6 decided he wanted a better view of the ocean, so he built a little addition on top of his house. This made the man very happy, but unfortunately it blocked the view of the mountains for his neighbors at house Number 5.

Not wanting to look at a brick wall, the family at house Number 5 decided to build an extra floor so they could see the mountains again – and from a much better angle than before. Now the views from house Number 5 and house Number 6 were perfect, but the old lady at house Number 4 could no longer see the forest.

It seemed every time someone built an addition

onto their home, someone else lost their view.

No one was willing to give up their view either, so the building continued and the additions became bigger and taller, wider and longer.

After a year no one had a clear view of anything anymore.

Everyone was tired of building additions and still
not having a good view, so they all agreed to put

their houses back to the way they had been before.

Time passed peacefully until one day someone new moved into house Number 3. He became good friends with the man at house Number 8 and visited him often.

He grew fond of the view of the green fields there. In fact . . .

the man from house Number 3 was so taken with the view that he wanted it for himself, so he built a gigantic addition on the side of his house.

And soon there were so many additions that nobody
had a clear view of anything anymore.